A Plain and Perfect Love

Amish Healer Series Book Two

Mary Lantz

Disclaimer

This story is a work of fiction, any resemblance to people is purely coincidence. All places, names, events, businesses, etc. are used in a fictional manner. All characters are from the imagination of the author.

Table of Contents

A Free book

Would you like a free story?

Claim Amish Special Delivery Here

**https://dl.bookfunnel.com/t9mmo3b6
rs**

Chapter One

Lavina shut the door between the medical practice and the kitchen with a firm tug, smiling as the latch clicked into place. She gave a great sigh of relief, rolling her stiff shoulders as she drew the chain lock over the door.

It always felt gut to end the day and retreat into the house, with nee more patients to see or remedies to mix. She loved helping her husband Samuel with his practice, but she also loved closing the door and spending time with her family.

As she turned away from the door and into the kitchen, her fingers trailed lightly across the raised scar tissue that ran along her cheek and jaw.

The motion was almost absentminded, a habit that came from a time that felt so long ago and far away from where her life was now.

It had been years since her terrible accident and the treatment that had brought her closer to Samuel, and even though she still bore some of the faint scars, it felt as if it had happened to some other person.

Her life now was so different and she didn't recognize the scared, traumatized young maedel she had been back then.

She could hear Samuel across the house, his heavy boots echoing on the wood floor of the nursery as he moved around the room. She smiled softly to herself as she opened a cabinet and took down a small bowl and spoon.

Life was full of so much joy these days -- the practice was thriving and their family was growing. She had nothing to complain about, and many things to thank Gott for blessing her with.

Footsteps in the doorway that led deeper into the house made her glance up, and she grinned as her husband came into the kitchen, their son nestled against his chest.

The one-year-old boy had a head of dark curls and cheeks rosy from his afternoon nap. Jacob gripped his father's shirt with a small fist, his eyes still bleary with sleep.

He was a healthy, fine-looking young boy and Lavina felt a surge of affection and love as she watched her husband and son cross the room and sit down at the kitchen table.

Samuel kicked his long legs out, settling Jacob more firmly in his lap.

The little boy sat up, peering around the room with large brown eyes becoming more and more bright as he woke up. When he spotted Lavina, he gave a happy laugh and reached his chubby arms toward her.

Moving across the room, she snatched her apron off the hook on the wall and went to fetch the boppoli's food from the counter where she had sieved it earlier in the day.

She set the bowl, spoon, and pot of food onto the table and reached behind her waist to tie the apron strings. Jacob continued to reach for her, making soft grunting noises as he fought against his father's grip. Samuel laughed, tickling his son lightly with affection.

"Now, now, little man," he said, his deep voice rumbling with laughter. "Let your Maemm tie her apron, gut-ness knows she's going to need it with the mess you always make at supper time."

Lavina laughed, pulling a chair closer to the table and sitting down next to her husband. She dipped the spoon into the boppoli's food, offering it to Jacob with a smile.

He lunged forward, almost throwing himself out of his father's hands in his excitement to eat. Samuel tightened his hold around the boy's waist, and Lavina carefully popped the spoon in Jacob' mouth.

The three of them sat quietly, the only sound the light smacking of Jacob' mouth as he ate the sieved food and the scrape of the spoon against the bowl.

After Jacob' initial hunger had subsided and he was eating at a much slower pace, Samuel cleared his throat.

"There's a new patient coming by tomorrow," he said, his eyes still on his son. "The family name is Lehman, have you heard of them? They've only just moved to Berlin last month."

"Ja, I've heard the name mentioned here and there in the past weeks," Lavina said, glancing at her husband and waiting for him to continue. She could tell that something was bothering him by the way his brow furrowed with worry.

"It's the mother and father, and their seventeen-year-old daughter Mildred," he said, his voice soft. "There was a terrible house fire, and their youngest died in the flames. A little girl named Betty, so I hear. It was a terrible blow for all of them, I think they made the move to start fresh."

Lavina paused, the spoon hanging in the air between her and Jacob. Her heart broke as she thought of that poor family, and the loss of their child.

"Oh, that is terrible," she breathed, blinking as Jacob batted at her arm. She moved the spoon closer to his mouth and waited as he took a bite. "That poor family. But why would they be patients?"

"It's just the daughter, Mildred is her name," Samuel said. "She was injured fairly badly in the fire and has scarring on her face. I know they've seen an English doctor, unfortunately due to her injuries she has some scarring. They are hoping I can help. Her father was injured as well -- he lost his leg just below the knee when a beam fell on him as he tried to save little Betty."

Lavina closed her eyes, trying to keep the tears from falling. She couldn't bear to think of the pain this family must be dealing with.

She knew some small part of their physical pain, having gone through her own trauma of burning and healing.

It had been a dark time in her life, and she couldn't imagine how much more painful it would have been if she had also lost someone she loved dearly.

A sudden compulsion to help the Lehmans in any way that she could came upon her, and she knew that it must be Gott using her to comfort them.

"Oh, Samuel," she breathed, setting the spoon into the bowl and catching up Jacob from his lap. She used her apron to wipe his little face and then snuggled him against her chest. "What can we do to help them? I feel as if Gott is telling me that I am needed to help them."

Samuel smiled lovingly at his wife, reaching out to grip her shoulder.

"I was hoping you would feel that way, Lavina," he said. "From what I hear, Mildred is a fair bit depressed because of her injuries and the amount of scarring. And I can't even get her father to come to see me. I'm hoping if we can help Mildred, even just a little, we might be able to convince her Daedd to come for treatment too. Helping this family is the neighborly thing to do."

"And maybe I can introduce Mildred to some of the young people in the community," Lavina said, the wheels in her mind turning. "Perhaps some of the eligible young men? There is much more than looks needed in a gut and Gottly wife, and that might help her regain some confidence."

"You are a wonder," Samuel laughed, leaning forward to kiss her cheek. "But you might want to pray for Gott's guidance before you set about match-making, Lavina Graber."

Lavina laughed, hugging Jacob more tightly against her. She would pray for Gott's guidance, but she just knew that this is what He meant for her to do. She would help Mildred Lehman realize that her worth was so much more than what she looked like.

Chapter Two

The November morning was crisp, but the sun was beginning to shine brightly in the sky. Despite the warmth of its rays, Mildred Lehman pulled her shawl tighter around her head, crossing the ends under her chin and tugging the edges so that her cheeks were hidden in the folds.

Her long, thick hair was like two dark curtains on either side of her face, covered by the thick wool of the shawl. She had knit the shawl herself, using a favorite shade of cornflower blue wool. Reaching her long fingers beneath it, she tucked her kapp strings into the folds.

She was glad for the cool breeze that blew up the hill as she walked along the road that led to the Graber house.

Her fingers twitched at her side, but she kept herself from running her fingertips across the ridges of scar tissue that marred the left side of her face.

It had become a nervous habit ever since she had been injured, and she wished that she could stop herself from doing it altogether. It was a constant reminder of the fire that had killed her sister, just a boppoli, and had left her father crippled and unable to work the family dairy farm.

She couldn't understand why Gott had allowed such a terrible tragedy to happen to a Gottly family like hers, and she was desperately trying not to turn away from Him.

But the constant reminder of her scars and her painful limp meant that it was impossible to forget the reason why they had moved away from the only community she had ever known.

Mildred felt the familiar tightening of her chest when she thought about the community they had left behind.

She missed her friends and neighbors desperately, and the comfort of a place that was so familiar to her.

Berlin and the surrounding community seemed strange and foreign to her, with new roads and businesses to remember and new people to meet.

She wondered if she would ever make friends, what with her terrible scarring. Who would want to be friends with someone who looked as if they could scare children?

She knew that sometimes terrible things happened to gut people, and she knew that it did not mean that Gott was punishing them. But sometimes that was the only thing that made sense, even if she knew it to be untrue.

She tried to be like her mother, so calm and accepting despite her grief. But it was so hard.

Her father had taken a job doing detail work at an Amish-owned furniture factory in Berlin that catered to the English tourists.

They had a need for someone to do the fine detail work on their finished pieces, and such a job meant that he didn't need his legs to work.

He could sit at a workstation and carve, using his wheelchair to move around a piece. He spent his days making beautiful carvings on furniture and wooden boxes -- work so intricate that it was already in high demand.

It was gut, honest work doing something he was skilled at, and Mildred was thankful for it. But she knew that he missed the dairy farm and his cows.

After the fire, and the loss of his leg, he wasn't able to work the farm or handle the cows and they had been forced to sell everything. She knew it pained her father, but he had been stoic and calm as the last cow had been trucked away.

He remained that way through the move, and even now he hardly said a word in complaint after starting his new job.

She could tell that the loss of his leg was more difficult than he let on, especially the lingering pain that made it difficult for him to walk with his crutch.

Which was why she was on her way to see Samuel Graber now, spending her morning trekking across the countryside.

Everyone in the community they had met said that she needed to see Samuel -- apparently, his wife Lavina had been through a terrible burning accident and that he had worked wonders for her.

Mildred was skeptical, but she figured that visiting the healer couldn't hurt.

It wasn't as if he could make her terrible scars any worse than they already were. And perhaps he could help -- either with the scarring or the lingering chronic pain that made it difficult to walk because of the scar tissue around her left knee.

Maybe if she went, she could convince her father to see him too. If Samuel Graber truly was the miracle worker that everyone said that he was, maybe he could help her father.

It had been so terrible for him in the English hospital, that she knew he didn't want to see another doctor for a long time.

At a slight bend in the road, the view opened up ahead of her and she saw a large white clapboard farmhouse set off the road.

It had a wide gravel drive that curved along the front of the house, and there were several buggies parked neatly in a row.

Beyond the house, a clothesline full of white linen stood out starkly against the grass. A hand-painted sign that said 'Samuel Graber -- Healing and Remedies' swung lightly in the breeze above the porch.

Mildred took a deep breath, squaring her shoulders as she walked up the drive.

The gravel crunched under her sensible black boots, and she tried to smooth the wrinkles from her skirt as she walked.

She reached up and checked her shawl, making sure that the folds of the shawl and her thick hair hid her scarred cheek from view. She knew that if anyone looked at her, they would see a pair of bright brown eyes peering out from underneath the shawl.

She felt a fluttering of nerves in her chest, but she knew that she needed to do this.

Seeing Samuel Graber was all anyone in Berlin could talk to her about, and she was tentatively hopeful that he could do something to help.

She climbed the porch steps and crossed the porch, reaching for the door handle of the large white-washed door that led into the medical practice.

Opening the door, she slipped inside a bright waiting room. The walls were painted a bright white, with refinished old pine floors that glowed with a fresh wax coating.

There were comfortable chairs set against the wall, and most of them were empty except for two. A man with a bandaged arm and a pained look on his face sat in one, and the other was occupied by a woman who held a wriggling child in her lap.

The little one had a badly burned hand, and Mildred watched as the mother tried to keep the child from using it to touch anything.

The little girl reached out toward a table that held a small stack of magazines and books, but the mother gently batted her hand away.

She nodded politely in greeting when the adults glanced up at her and looked around the room.

Mildred sat in one of the chairs, knowing that the other two patients would surely be seen before she did.

She crossed her ankles, straightening and smoothing her skirt. She let her bag slide off her shoulder, reaching in to pull out her knitting.

It was a small project using the pretty cornflower blue yarn her cousin had sent her before the move, and the color made Mildred smile softly.

She untangled the yarn with her fingers, and then picked up her needles. Knitting the first stitch, she tried to settle her racing heart as she prepared to wait to see the healer everyone spoke so highly about.

Chapter Three

Henry Schrock set the pail of milk down gently, careful not to spill a drop onto the packed earth floor of the cavernous milking barn.

The long row of cows stretched toward the far end of the building, their large bodies shifting in the dim light from the casement windows.

The air was heavy with the rich smell of earth and dung, punctuated by the sharp tang of fresh milk. The sound of soft grunts and the whirr of the milking machines filled the air, and Henry reached up to wipe his brow with his shirtsleeve.

He could see his brother Mervin further down the row, his tall form almost lost among the tangle of tubes hooked up to the milking machines.

Henry stood up from his crouch and grinned, remembering his father's many grumbling complaints about the noise and bother of the machines.

Despite the fact that having the milking machines allowed their small family dairy farm to triple in size and production, he still thought the old ways were best.

If it had been up to him, he often said, the Amish communities should have never allowed the new technology to be used. Henry and his brother would just let him ramble and nod along, though privately they would chuckle to each other about how their father could never go back to hand milking all of his cows.

The new technology had done wonders for their efficiency.

"That's me done," he called to his brother, raising a hand to catch his attention. "I'm heading into the house."

Mervin glanced his way and waved in return, grinning back at his younger brother.

"Almost finished with this one and I'll be right behind you," he called. "Tell Maemm to save me some pancakes, will you?"

Henry laughed and began to walk down the row of cows toward the large doors that led out into the barnyard.

Pushing open the doors, he blinked as he walked out into the early morning sunlight. It took several moments for his eyes to get used to the brightness of the sun -- he had been in the dimly lit barn for hours.

The yard was quiet at this time of the day, with almost everyone either in the milking barns or in the house eating breakfast.

Henry liked to be out in the yard when it was so still and serene, with the sun coming up between the buildings and casting long shadows on the ground.

Soon there would be a commotion of wagons and horses and people as everyone loaded the wagons and prepared for the day's milk deliveries.

After breakfast, Henry would be driving a wagon into Berlin to do his round of deliveries. He was looking forward to his favorite delivery, to the Amish-owned coffeeshop Berlin Beans in the center of town.

His friend Marshall owned the coffee shop, and Henry enjoyed spending a moment chatting with him and drinking a cup of coffee.

Sometimes he would see other friends there and he would hear more of the news from throughout the community.

As he entered the house and took the stairs up to the upper floor, he thought about the maedel he would sometimes see at the coffee shop.

There wasn't any one particular girl he was interested in these days -- he used to think that he was in love with Rebecca Zook, but it had been a passing fancy.

He realized that it was just a crush when she had chosen Freeman Lapp to court her, though he had to admit that he had been surprised at her choice.

Henry didn't think he was vain, but he did know from the reactions of the maedel that he was considered one of the best-looking young men in the community.

He walked into the bathroom that he shared with his brothers and washed his hands. Setting out his shaving kit, he prepared his face and began to shave.

As the razor slid along his sculpted jaw, he considered himself in the small mirror that hung above the sink.

He had a strong jaw and high cheekbones, with lightly tanned skin and a shock of blond hair that was always falling into his wide blue eyes.

He tried not to let his looks go to his head, though he did take extra care to always make sure he looked his best.

As he finished shaving, he dried his face with a towel and thought about how much more handsome he would be when he was married and allowed to grow a beard.

But for that to happen, he would need to find a gut wife, and that was harder than he had ever anticipated.

Most of the maedel in town could barely string two words together when he was around, collapsing into a puddle of giggles and blushes the minute his blue eyes turned their way.

He supposed he should have found it flattering, but really it was just annoying. He didn't want a simpering fool for a wife -- he wanted someone who was intelligent and could hold a conversation.

And, someone who had a gut head for business on her shoulders and could help him run the dairy farm.

She didn't have to know much about cows, he could teach her all that, but she needed to have a quick mind and the ability for hard work.

He left the bathroom and bounded down the stairs. Walking into the kitchen, he kissed his mother on the cheek before moving towards the kitchen table.

Plates piled high with steaming pancakes were waiting for him, and he felt his stomach grumble with hunger. His mother was one of the best cooks in the community, and it was his hope that whatever maedel he did find for his wife would be just as gut.

He said gut-morning to his father and brothers, picking up a plate and serving himself. As he walked to his seat, he couldn't help checking his hair in the small mirror his mother kept hung by the back door.

"Man looks on the outward appearance, but the Lord looks on the heart," his mother said, shaking a spatula in his general direction with a pointed look.

Henry grinned sheepishly at being caught and sank into a chair at the table, setting his plate in front of him. He rolled his eyes at his brothers, who were all laughing at him.

"Love is patient and kind," he retorted gut-naturedly, laughing as his mother chuckled at his wit. She shook her head, turning back to the stove with a sigh. Henry was gut-natured and kind if a bit vain. He would learn soon enough that it wasn't what a person looked like, but what they did and said that counted.

Chapter Four

"Mildred Lehman?"

A slender woman with thick auburn hair and a wide smile stepped through the door that led into the exam room.

She wore a pristine white kapp on her head, the strings hanging down to frame a heart-shaped face. Stepping into the room, she stuck her hand out toward Mildred with a grin.

"My name is Lavina Graber," the woman said, her voice warm. "You are very welcome here! We were excited to hear that a new family had moved into the area, and look forward to getting to know you better."

Mildred nodded politely, grasping Lavina's hand softly.

So this was Lavina Graber, the wife of the healer and the woman whose scars he had healed. Mildred tried not to be obvious about staring at the older girl's face, but a soft, knowing smile came across Lavina's face.

"Come on back," she said, motioning toward the door. "Samuel is ready for you now."

Mildred rose from her chair, straightening her skirt with nervous hands as she followed Lavina through the door.

Beyond it was a large open space, lined with shelves that groaned under the weight of glass bottles and labeled boxes.

Two desks were positioned facing each other toward the back of the room, both crowded with papers and supplies. An exam table sat in the middle of the room, draped with a clean white sheet.

Lavina ushered her to the exam table and pressed her gently to sit on it, standing close by and smiling as Mildred made herself comfortable.

She glanced back up at Lavina once she was sitting down, her eyes roving over the other girl's face.

"You can still see some of it here," Lavina said with a soft smile, her fingers tracing along her jawline. "Samuel and old healer Mast did wonders on it, but not even they could get rid of the scars completely."

Mildred flushed, embarrassed to be caught staring. She ducked her head, stammering an apology.

"It's absolutely fine," Lavina said gently, reaching out to grasp the younger girl's hand. "I know exactly what you are going through, and I know how valuable it would have been for me if I had known someone who had gone through the same thing I was dealing with. I know that you have pain and grief that I never had to suffer, but I can at least help you with the physical scarring."

Mildred let her eyes raise to Lavina's face once again, and she sucked in a ragged breath.

"How did he do it?"

Lavina opened her mouth to answer, but a deep voice cut her off.

"With patience and skill," a stocky man said, striding across the room as he wiped his hands dry on a clean white cotton towel. "And buckets of our special burn salve."

Mildred's eyes widened as she watched the man peck a quick kiss on Lavina's cheek before coming to stand next to the exam table.

So this must be Samuel Graber -- he was so young!

He was of an age to his wife, which surprised Mildred. As much as everyone praised his skill as a healer, she had assumed he would be older and with more experience.

"Gut dag, Mildred," he said, smiling gently as he watched her. "My name is Samuel Graber and I am very glad to meet you." He set the towel he had been drying his hands with onto the table beside the exam table. "Would you kindly take off your shawl so that I may see the extent of your injury?"

Mildred felt a dread rush through her, chilling her blood. She knew that she had to show the healer her scars, but it was hard to open herself up to the looks and stares she knew would come when people saw how disfigured she truly was.

With shaking fingers, she pushed back her shawl until it fell against her back.

Lavina stepped closer and reached out, taking Mildred's hand in hers.

Her hand was warm and comforting, and she squeezed lightly in support as Samuel pushed back Mildred's curtains of hair.

She squeezed her eyes shut tightly, not wanting to see the pity in Samuel's eyes as he examined her scars.

Several quiet moments passed and Mildred found herself curious. She opened her eyes and watched Samuel's face as his warm hand gently gripped her chin, turning her face this way and that.

His eyes weren't full of sympathy, as she had expected, but with a warm gentleness that began to put her at ease.

When Samuel's gentle fingertips traced a particularly nasty scar across her jaw, Mildred flushed with shame and closed her eyes. A tear escaped and she felt it track down her disfigured skin. She knew how ugly the scarring was, and she truly felt like a monster with half of her face melting away.

Mildred jumped in surprise as Samuel laid his entire palm across her cheek, the warmth of his skin sending a tingling sensation through her. She watched his face with wide eyes, curious as he stared at her face intently.

"I think I can help reduce the scarring," he said, his voice almost absentminded as he watched her. "They won't vanish completely, but I think we can reduce them and soften their appearance. A combination of the burn salve with some simple exercises to soften the scars and strengthen the tissue should help immensely."

Mildred felt her breath catch in her throat. Could it be true?

"I noticed that you were limping when you walked into the exam room," Lavina said softly. "Was your leg injured as well?"

"Ja, my left leg was burned fairly badly," Mildred said, nodding her head. "The scarring around my knee makes the leg stiff and painful."

Samuel listened to her explanation and then nodded, taking a slight step back. He asked her to sit further back on the exam table, bringing her legs up to extend out in front of her.

When both legs were up on the table, he moved back to her side and reached out to take her left leg in his hands.

For several moments he ran his hands over her knee and down her shin, the sweeping motions of his palms leaving a tingling warmth in their wake.

After several moments, Samuel finally stopped and stepped back with a smile. He reached out and helped her to stand, steadying her as she stood stiffly beside the exam table.

"Put more weight on that left leg," he said, watching as she did what he asked.

Mildred shifted slightly, her eyes widening as she glanced up at Samuel.

"Does it feel better?"

She nodded, unable to speak. Her leg didn't feel half as stiff as it had this morning and placed her weight onto it wasn't painful.

"How did you do that?"

Samuel grinned at her, his eyes twinkling.

"I have a Gott-given talent," he said. "Every skill I possess comes directly from Him." He bustled away, toward a table at the back of the room. "I want you to take home this pot of burn salve and spread it on all of your scars nightly. Lavina will show you some exercises you can do to help your face and your leg, and I want you to come by at least three times a week for hands-on treatment. After several months of all this, I think we will see great improvement."

Mildred was wide-eyed and speechless as Lavina and Samuel said gut-bye, her wave half-hearted as she stepped out into the late morning sunshine. Her mind was whirling with possibilities and half-formed thoughts, and for the first time since the fire she dared to hope.

Chapter Five

Lavina set the dinner plate with its heaping serving of casserole on the table in front of Samuel and smiled as he thanked her. Stepping back from the table, she wiped her hands on her apron and then reached behind her to untie it.

Hanging the apron on the hook on the wall, she paused at the door from the kitchen into the main part of the house, tilting her head and listening for a moment.

Satisfied that Jacob was still sleeping soundly, she walked to the counter and picked up her own plate. She sat next to her husband, reaching to take his hand as he led them in their mealtime prayer.

After they had each said their silent prayer to Gott, she watched with affectionate pride as Samuel tucked into his casserole with excitement.

It always warmed her heart to see her husband enjoy her cooking so much, and she received so much pleasure from finding new dishes to surprise him with.

This casserole had been a new recipe she had begged from one of the older women at church, and it was obviously a big hit.

"This is amazing, Lavina," he said after swallowing a bite. "You need to borrow more recipes from Mrs. Zook.

She grinned, taking a bite and agreeing with Samuel. It really was very gut!

They ate in companionable silence for several moments, before Samuel set his fork down and sighed.

"Mildred Lehman came in for her treatment while you were running errands earlier," he said, his brow creasing a bit with worry. He sat back in his chair and ran a hand over his face, looking extremely tired and worn down.

"Why do you look so anxious, Samuel? You said she has been doing well with the exercises and burn ointment," Lavina said, watching him carefully.

She loved how compassionate her husband was, but she worried that sometimes he let himself become too close and involved with his patients and it caused him to worry.

"Oh, she has," he said, waving a hand. He sat up a bit, smiling as he thought of the younger maedel. "She follows every instruction I give her, and I really do think it is helping. She can't see it yet, but the scars are softening."

"Then what has you so worried?"

He ran an anxious hand through his hair and sat back in his chair again, crossing his arms over his wide chest. He sat quietly for a moment, thinking about what he wanted to say.

"It's her attitude," he said. "Do you remember how you were when I first started coming to treat your burns?"

Lavina stilled, her mind going back to that awful time. It felt so far away, and she disliked remembering how deep into a depression she had fallen.

She had felt so lost and alone, trapped in her bed by her injuries and certain that Gott was punishing her. The depression had been almost unbearable.

"I remember," she said softly, smiling as Samuel reached out to clasp her hand. "But you soon dragged me out of it, kicking and screaming. I can never say denke enough."

He chuckled, squeezing her hand lightly.

"Well, how you were is how I find Mildred now," he said, the worry coming back to his expression. "She is quiet and reserved, but I sense a deep well of anxiety and fear beneath the surface. I don't think she will allow herself to close herself off completely -- she's too worried about her parents, her father especially. I think she feels responsible for them and she knows they worry about her. But, of course, she doesn't want them to worry, so she pretends to be fine. But she is hurting, I can see it plain as day."

"I've noticed that she still hides her face when I see her out in the community," Lavina said. "I think much of what worries her is how other people will react to her injuries."

"Yes, her self-esteem is very low," Samuel said.

"I think she avoids meeting anyone new or even holding conversations with anyone outside her family and immediate circle. It's as if the burns have crippled her ability to talk to people."

Lavina stood up and picked up her and Samuel's plates, taking them to the sink. As she filled the basin with water, she looked out the window at the darkening sky. There were giant clouds on the horizon, and the wind was picking up. It looked as if a storm was coming, and she wondered if there was snow in the forecast.

"I remember what it was like to feel so ugly you could barely look at anyone," Lavina said, her voice pensive. "It felt as if Gott had turned His face away from me, and I was in constant darkness. It took you loving me to show me that Gott had never once abandoned me, that He had always been there. I think what Mildred needs is someone to love her for who she is, burns and all. Someone who can see the Gottly, talented young woman she truly is."

Samuel rose from his chair and came to stand next to his wife, leaning his hip against the counter as he watched her begin to wash the dishes.

He picked up a clean dish towel and took a bowl she handed to him, drying it off carefully.

"I can already see where this is going," he chuckled. "You're going to turn match-maker and try to find Mildred the perfect husband."

He laughed and dodged the dish towel she snapped at him playfully, holding his hands up in surrender.

"I didn't say it was a bad idea! I just know you too well," he said.

She smiled at him, turning back to the dishes with a self-deprecating laugh.

"Ja, well," she said, with a playful huff. "You can't tell me that Mildred Lehman isn't a lovely, Gottly young woman who deserves someone who will appreciate her. There just has to be the right man out there who will love her for who she is, not what she looks like."

"And I'm willing to bet you already have a list of prospects?"

She swatted at him again and laughed as he snatched the dishtowel from her hand.

"There aren't many eligible young men of an age that would suit," she said, leaning against the counter and folding her arms across her chest. "What about your brother?"

"Leroy? Oh no, he would never do," Samuel laughed. "He's so quiet that neither of them would ever say a word to each other.

"You're right, of course," she said. "That leaves David Gingerich, Emmanuel Bontranger, Paul Yoder..."

"What about Henry Schrock? He's unattached and I've heard that he's looking for someone to help him run the dairy operations," Samuel said.

"Oh no, not Henry," Lavina said, wrinkling her nose and shaking her head. "He is a gut man, but he is a little too vain. I don't know if he is the right person for Mildred."

"Well, I'm sure you'll find her the perfect husband," Samuel said, leaning over to kiss his wife on the cheek. "Just be careful, Lavina. We wouldn't want Mildred to get hurt in the process."

Chapter Six

Henry tugged lightly on the reins as the horse slowed down in front of Berlin Beans coffee shop in downtown Berlin. The wagon came to a complete stop and he jumped down, looping the reins around the hitching post next to the sidewalk.

He glanced down the street, making sure there was no traffic before walking around the wagon with a quick step.

At the back of the wagon, he lifted a crate of milk and stepped up onto the sidewalk. The morning was getting on and the sun was high in the sky -- even though the air was crisp and cool, the sun's rays were warm on his face.

He tipped his face up and took a deep breath, enjoying the warmth as much as he could. Snow would be here soon before he knew it.

The bell over the door jangled merrily as he pushed his way into the coffee shop. Inside he breathed in the rich smell of coffee beans as the warmth and noise of the shop surrounded him.

There were several customers seated at the round cafe tables, their voices a steady drone over the noises from behind the counter. A young Amish maedel was at the cash register, smiling at an English tourist couple who were reading the menu.

It seemed to be a fairly busy morning, and Henry smiled happily. He liked to see the business doing well, for his friend Marshall's sake.

Henry shouldered the crate and moved to the back of the shop, rounding the counter and nodding at the girl. She gave him a shy wave, a deep blush rising to fill her round cheeks.

She looked away, shifting slightly where she stood. Henry felt a sinking feeling, hating how girls could barely even look at him without turning into a simpering mess. With a frustrated sigh, he walked back into the open kitchen.

Marshall Miller, the owner of Berlin Beans and one of Henry' gut friends, came out of the back office with a grin. He took one look at the sour expression on Henry face and chuckled, waving for him to put the crate down on a large preparation table.

"What is it this time, Henry? Did you dare to say hello to poor, sweet Maggie? You know she can't handle it," he laughed, clapping his friend on the back.

Henry glowered at Marshall, leaning against the table with a huff.

"Silly little thing," he grumbled. "Can't even look me in the face without turning beet red."

"Poor Henry," Marshall guffawed. "So handsome that he is too handsome, and scares all the girls away."

Henry rolled his eyes, swatting gut-naturedly at his friend. Marshall grinned, looking over the milk delivery with a practiced eye.

"This all looks gut, as usual," he said. "Come out to the front and let me make you a coffee. It's been a bit since you've been in, it will be gut to catch up."

Henry followed Marshall back into the front of the shop. As Marshall went to make him a coffee, he wandered over to a wall lined with shelves.

There was the usual display of coffee mugs made by local potters, but the most amazing display of knitted handmade gifts was tucked onto several shelves. Scarves, purses, mittens, and even little stuffed animals. Henry picked up a beautifully made little cat, with a curled knitted tail and tiger stripes.

It was intricately made with immense skill, and he knew immediately that his mother would love it. Her birthday was coming up, and this was just the thing.

He walked back to the front of the shop, leaning his hip against the counter as he continued to look at the small knitted cat.

Maggie was still at the cash register, but she was helping another customer. Henry waited for Marshall, who soon join him holding two mugs of coffee. He noticed what Henry was holding and grinned happily.

"I see you've found my newest acquisition," he said, nodding toward an empty table.

The two men walked over and sat down. Henry set the cat on the table in front of him, nodding his thanks as Marshall handed him a coffee.

"It's impressive work," he said, taking a sip.

"They're made by an Amish maedel who just moved here from another community," Marshall said, waving toward the display. "She's very talented and has a gut head on her shoulders. Really knows how to bargain, that one. She talked us into taking a lower percentage of the sales, just at first to see how well they do with the tourists. Her name is Mildred, she moved here with her mother and father."

Henry sat chatting with Marshall for a while, drinking their coffee and enjoying the morning. When one of his employees called for Marshall from the kitchen, Henry got up and went back over to the display of knitted items.

He knew he wanted to get his mother the little cat, but she would also like one of the small knitted purses.

He opened a flowered one and looked approvingly at the lined interior, with a number of small compartments for money and things.

He was just about to take the two items to the cash register when the bell above the door rang and a maedel stepped into the shop.

She was tall and slender, dressed in a dark wool dress with a basket over one arm. Thick, dark hair spilled over her shoulders and hung over her face in two shining curtains.

He could see her kapp strings tangled in her hair, but the kapp itself was hidden beneath a beautiful knitted lace shawl that was wrapped around her head. Her face was in shadow, hidden behind her hair and the shawl.

It was a cool November day, but it wasn't exceptionally cold. Henry wondered why she was so bundled up, but thought that maybe she felt the chill more than other people would because she was so thin.

Marshall came striding out from behind the counter with a smile.

"Mildred! We were just talking about your beautiful creations," he said, waving the girl over. "My friend Henry here is going to buy something for his mother."

Henry smiled politely at the maedel, holding out his selections.

"Gut dag," he said. "You do very beautiful work, I think my mother will especially love this sweet little cat. I was glad to hear that you were able to get a gut deal out of Marshall, he is usually a bit of a skinflint."

Marshall pretended to be affronted, which made Mildred chuckle. Henry could see a faint blush on her pale cheeks, and her eyes were large and brown as they watched him from behind her hair.

They peered at him, and he felt as if he was being measured and observed. It wasn't an unpleasant feeling, just one he wasn't used to. This girl wasn't the simpering, blushing type who could barely speak to him.

"Denke, for the compliment on my work," she said, her voice soft and rich. "And for the compliment on my negotiating skills. A maedel must have a gut head for business these days if she is to sell her wares to discerning tourists."

She smiled at Henry and then turned to Marshall, setting her basket on the counter.

Henry went to the cash register and paid for the two knitted items, waiting as Maggie wrapped them in brightly-colored tissue paper. The whole while, he watched Mildred as she talked with Marshall. There was a girl with a gut head on her shoulders. It would be interesting to know more about her.

Chapter Seven

Mildred dipped her fingers into the pot of burn salve and then gently swiped it over her jaw, spreading the thick salve up her cheekbone to cover her facial scars.

A tingling sensation spread throughout her skin where the salve touched, and it felt gut to rub the remedy into the scar tissue. She turned her face this way and that, peering at her reflection in the small mirror above the bathroom sink.

She thought that maybe there was a little bit of improvement to the appearance of the scars, but she couldn't be sure. And she hated to get her hopes up, only to have them dashed once again.

But, she could admit that the salve was working wonders for the scarring on her knee -- she could feel them becoming softer and more supple, and less restrictive of her movement.

The muscles were no longer tight and painful, and she was able to do the exercises Samuel had taught her with much more ease. Her limp was becoming less and less pronounced, and if improvement continued the way it was, she hoped to be able to walk without a limp within a few months.

Mildred went to see Samuel Graber three to four times a week, and she had to believe it was helping. She could definitely feel an improvement, but she was terrified that any lessening of her physical scars was just a trick of her mind.

What if she was meant to be disfigured forever? What if the scars on her face were permanent?

She shook her head, trying to shake away bad thoughts. Placing the pot of burn salve back on the shelf, she reached up and straightened her kapp with a decisive tug.

She took a deep breath, willing herself to forget her troubles.

She was heading downstairs to have lunch with her parents and she couldn't give them any reason to worry. They had so many other things on their mind -- the still-new, grief of losing a child, her father's injuries, a new home, and community -- and she hated the idea of them worrying over her too.

She took one last look at herself in the small mirror and then turned to exit the bathroom. She walked across the landing and down the stairs, heading into the kitchen where she could hear her mother preparing the meal.

Her father was sitting at the kitchen table, his wheelchair pulled up to the edge of the table. He had his accounting book spread open in front of him, a sight that was so normal to Mildred that she felt herself relax a little, despite the anxiety.

It was gut to see her father doing the things he had always done to take care of them all, even if his injuries made things different.

She crossed the room and leaned down to kiss her father on the cheek, smiling as he patted her face affectionately. She sat down in the chair beside him, pulling herself up to the table.

Her mother set a bowl of soup with a thick slice of buttered bread on the table in front of her with a smile.

"You look cheerful this morning, Mildred," her mother said, picking up a bowl and setting it in front of her husband. "It's gut to see you back in such high spirits."

"It's a gut day, Maemm," Mildred said, smiling at her mother. She was glad that her mother couldn't see the anxiety that still bubbled up beneath the surface.

Her mother sat across from Mildred and her father at the table, her own bowl of soup in front of her. She reached across the table and took her husband and her daughter's hand and they all bowed their heads as each gave thanks silently over the meal.

Once he was finished, Mildred's mother looked across the table at her daughter with a searching expression.

"How have the treatments with Samuel Graber been coming along?"

Mildred set her spoon down beside her bowl and glanced up.

"They seem to be going well," she said, her voice hesitant. "Samuel says that I am improving daily and that he can see much improvement since I started seeing him."

"And what do you see?"

Her father looked at her shrewdly, his dark eyes sharp as he waited for her to answer his question.

"I'm not sure," she said quietly. "Some days I feel as if I can see what Samuel sees, and others I'm not so sure. I do know that the scarring around my knee is feeling much better and it's easier to move and walk. That truly does seem to be improving."

"That's wonderful! Your mobility is the most important thing," her mother said, glancing at her husband. He smiled at her, and then looked at his daughter.

"Your mother is right," he said. "The most important thing to heal is your ability to walk without pain. Everything else is just vanity."

Mildred ducked her head, feeling a rush of shame wash over her. She felt her father place a warm hand on her shoulder, giving it a light squeeze.

"I know that how you look is important to young maedels," he said. "It is normal to want to look your best, but it is important to remember that it isn't your looks that Gott values. It is your heart and your character."

"I know, Daedd," Mildred said, her eyes still downcast. "But I can't help wishing that Samuel could do something about the scarring on my face. What young man would ever want to marry a woman who looks like this?"

"Mildred, you must listen to your father," her mother said, her voice warm and kind. "He is right -- Gott values what is inside of you, not your outward appearance. And any truly Gottly young man would see past your scarring to the wonderful young woman you are. A man who is put off by your injuries isn't worth wanting anyway."

Mildred nodded, smiling at her mother and father. As they began to chat about her father's job as an artisan woodcarver and the gossip from around the community, she ate her soup quietly.

She thought about what her parents had said, and about how she had been allowing her scars to dictate her mood and behavior.

She wasn't sure that she could just forget about them or ignore them, but she hoped that she could learn to accept them if that is what Gott meant for her.

She said a silent prayer asking Gott to lay his hands on Samuel so that he could heal her to the best of his abilities. She asked Gott to guide him and for Him to free her from as much pain as He wished to.

Mildred still wasn't completely sure why Gott had allowed such a tragedy to happen to a gut, Gottly family such as hers, but she prayed that she could learn to accept his will, even if she didn't understand it.

Chapter Eight

Henry watched as Mildred Lehman chatted quietly with Marshall at the counter of the Berlin Beans coffee shop. He had the perfect view from his table by the window, where he sat with a large mug of fresh coffee.

His deliveries were finished for the day, and he was enjoying a moment of quiet before driving the wagon back home to get started on his afternoon work on the dairy farm.

Mildred walked to the shelf that held her knitted guts and stood looking at it for a moment.

Henry had noticed earlier that the shelves were looking rather bare, and Marshall had exclaimed that they could hardly keep anything in stock.

The little knitted gifts sold so quickly that Mildred was in the shop twice a week with new guts to put out. He assumed that was what she was currently here for, and it was confirmed when she slipped the basket she held off her arm and began placing new little knitted items on the shelves.

He admitted to himself that he was intrigued by Mildred. She still kept her shawl wrapped tightly around her head, her pale face always in shadow behind the edge of the shawl and her kapp..

He had noticed that her limp seemed to be getting better. He was so curious about the quiet, reserved maedel, but she wasn't very forthcoming with details about her life.

In the past few weeks, he had chatted with her when he happened to be at the coffee shop when she came in.

They talked about business things, about how she started making items to sell and what her goals were, about his plans for the dairy farm. She told him that her father used to run a dairy farm where they lived before moving to Berlin, but when he asked her more about it she had clammed up.

Henry couldn't understand why she was so hesitant to talk more about her life, but at least she was talking to him at all.

Mildred had blushed during their first meeting, but he thought it was most likely because he had complimented her, and not because she was like the other simpering young girls who could barely speak to him.

In fact, she seemed to have nee problem looking him in the eyes and talking to him. It was refreshing, and it endeared him to her even more.

He set his empty coffee mug down on the table and pushed his chair back, standing up. He walked over to the shelf and stood beside it, smiling as he greeted Mildred.

She smiled back at him, setting a beautiful knit hat on the shelf.

"Gut dag, Mildred," he said, his eyes roaming over the items she was placing on the shelves. There were more winter things this time -- hats and mittens, plush scarves in beautiful stripes, socks that looked very warm. "The new things look beautiful. I'm sure they will be bestsellers just like the things you brought last week."

She smiled and blushed, her eyes sliding to the shelves with a hint of pride. When she caught him noticing her, she ducked her head.

"Denke, Henry, that's so nice of you to say," she said. "I thought with the weather turning a bit cooler, it was time to bring in the winter things. I hope everyone likes the hats, I really enjoy making them."

"I'm sure they will," he said, leaning against the wall next to the shelf. He watched her work for a moment, admiring each item she placed carefully on the shelf.

"What do you have planned for the day?"

Her questions caught him off guard, he had been enjoying the quiet and watching her work industriously.

He blinked, trying to pull his mind back to the present. It wasn't often that Mildred initiated a conversation with him -- he usually had to work at drawing her out of her shell with gentle questions.

He found that he liked the challenge, and once she grew more comfortable in the situation she was an interesting person to talk to.

"I'll be leaving here in a bit and heading back home to the dairy farm," he said. "My father is expecting a delivery of a few new cows, and there's a lot of work to prepare spaces for them."

She set a pair of mittens on the shelf and smiled, her eyes brightening at the mention of cows.

"Oh! We always loved when new cows would come," she said. "My sister and I would name them and tidy up their stalls so they would feel at home." Her expression darkened for a moment and she paused, taking a deep breath. "What sort of cows has your father ordered?"

"Holsteins, this time," he said, wondering what had caused her to pause. He thought he had seen a flash of pain in her eyes when she had mentioned her sister. "Hopefully they will be gut milkers!"

"Holsteins are such lovely cows," she said. "Daedd always said they were his favorite cows. But that was before the accident."

She trailed off, her expression closing off and her shoulders stiffening.

"Accident?"

At the sound of Henry voice, she straightened and looked toward the door. Henry could barely see her expression beneath her shawl and the tilt of her head, but he could just tell that it was blank and expressionless. She took a quick breath, staring toward the front of the shop for a moment before shaking herself lightly. She turned back to Henry and gave a stiff smile.

"I shouldn't keep my mother waiting in the buggy -- it was nice to see you, Henry," she said, catching up her basket and turning away from him.

He watched her leave, feeling confused. What had he said? She had obviously been suddenly uncomfortable, but he couldn't figure it out. Something had made her freeze like a captured wild animal.

There was something in her past that still pained her, he was sure of it. But he had nee idea what it could possibly be.

He wandered over to the counter, leaning his hip against it and crossing his arms over his chest. Marshall finished up with a customer at the register and then came to stand beside him. He noticed Henry staring toward the door with a pensive look on his handsome face.

"What's got you all flustered?"

Henry looked at his friend and shrugged.

"Do you know what sort of accident Mildred could have been talking about?"

"Accident? No, I don't think so," Marshall said, his expression thoughtful. "She doesn't talk much about her personal life and I haven't met anyone who knows anything about the family."

"Have you met her folks?"

"Nee," Marshall answered, shaking his head. "I haven't ever seen her father at all, though I hear he's taken a job carving specialty pieces at the woodshop. Her mother drives her into town and I've seen her from afar, but never met her."

"Don't you think it's curious that not any one seems to know anything about her or her family?"

Marshall shrugged, looking at his friend shrewdly.

"Everyone has their secrets, Henry," he said. "If Mildred ever wants to tell me about her family, she will. Until then, it isn't any of my business."

"There's a mystery there," Henry said, his brow furrowed.

"Why don't you just ask her about her family? The two of you seem to be friendly lately, you always chat together if you're both here," Marshall said. "And friends tell each other things. Something tells me that Mildred Lehman needs a friend."

Henry gazed at the door Mildred had slipped out of for several moments, letting Marshall's words tumble about in his mind. He also thought that Mildred needed a friend. He wanted to be her friend, but he wasn't very sure that she was ready to let him.

Chapter Nine

Mildred waved gut-bye to Henry as she walked out of the coffee shop. The cold air outside hit her face and she tugged her shawl tightly around her head and neck.

The wind tangled her skirt in her legs and she clutched her basket close to her body as she made her way to where her mother had parked the buggy.

It felt gut to have someone to chat with, even if they only ever talked about business. He seemed to have endless patience for her talk about knitting and selling artisan guts.

Henry was a kind man, and he listened thoughtfully as she explained her hopes and goals for her little knitting business.

He seemed to enjoy talking about the business of dairy farming with her too, and it was nice to be able to talk about something that had been a part of her life for so long.

She blushed to think about how seriously he took her ideas and advice -- it felt gut to have someone who respected her enough to take her seriously.

He was respectful of the boundaries she placed around her personal life, and for that she was grateful. She didn't want to have to talk about Betty's death or the tragic accident, and she had been so relieved when Henry had respected that.

Someday she might open up a bit more to him, especially now that they were definitely becoming friends. It felt so gut to finally make a friend in Berlin -- the Grabers were gut friends but they were in a different stage of their lives to Mildred.

Henry was of an age with her and thinking about the same things when it came to starting their businesses and lives.

She could appreciate that and liked how he always listened to her without patronizing her.

As she reached the buggy, she opened the door and climbed into the box. Her mother was waiting for her, watching as she settled herself on the seat and pulled a wool blanket over her lap.

When she was settled, her mother flicked the reins and the horse pulled ahead onto the road. They drove in silence for several minutes, Mildred staring out at the passing countryside.

"I saw that you were talking with that Henry boy again," her mother said suddenly.

Mildred glanced at her, her eyebrows raised in surprise.

"Ja, he was asking my opinion on some new cows his father had delivered last week," she said. "He's trying to talk his father into purchasing a few more and was asking a few questions about Daedd's ordering process back when we had our farm."

Her mother watched her carefully for a moment and then sighed.

"He is a very handsome young man," she said, her eyebrows raised so high they disappeared into her hair line.

Mildred sat up straighter in her seat and let out a breath.

"Is he? I hadn't noticed," she said, looking out the window.

But that was a fib -- of course, she had noticed. Henry sometimes looked like a carved Renaissance statue from a history book come to life. Sometimes his gut looks took her breath away. But she saw how silly other girls acted around him, and she saw how much it annoyed and hurt him. So she tried not to let his looks affect how she treated him.

"I don't believe that for a second," her mother chuckled. "He is too handsome to ignore."

"He might be, but that has nothing to do with why I am friends with him," Mildred said with a frown. She couldn't imagine deciding who she would be friends with based on how they looked!

Her mother tugged the reins lightly, slowing the horse down to a walk as they came to an intersection. Mildred hoped the distraction would stop this line of conversation she seemed intent on following.

She shifted in her seat, feeling uncomfortable and strange. She hadn't allowed herself to see Henry in any romantic way, because she knew that he would never find a maedel like her attractive. Someone as gut-looking as Henry would want a wife who was just as handsome as he was.

Once her mother had guided the horse through the intersection and they were once again trotting lightly down the road, she glanced at Mildred with a shrewd look.

"Don't you think he might be interested in you as more than just a friend?"

Mildred laughed, short and sharp. She shook her head, smiling at her mother.

"Nee, Maemm, I don't," she said, smiling ruefully. "There is nee way such a gut-looking young man would ever be interested in someone that looks like I do."

She gestured limply at the scars on her cheeks and turned to look out the window again. She felt tears pricking at the corners of her eyes and she blinked, staring blindly out at the passing fields.

Her mother was silent for several moments, the only sound the steady beat of the horse's hooves and the creaking of the buggy.

Mildred focused on her breaths, trying desperately to steady her racing heart.

"I have to admit that I'm a bit disappointed, Mildred," her mother said softly, her eyes never leaving the road. "I thought that your father and I had raised you to know that a person's worth is never based on their outward appearance. Everything that you have been taught speaks of the beauty of a person's soul, not the beauty of their face."

Mildred felt a crushing sense of shame press down upon her. She knew all of this -- but why was it so hard to ignore her injuries? She had never thought of herself as a vain person, but ever since the accident, she couldn't put aside the vanity of wanting to be rid of her scars.

"I know, Maemm," she whispered, her voice breaking in the stillness of the buggy. "I'm sorry to disappoint you."

Her mother glanced at her and then tugged lightly on the reins, steering the horse to the side of the road and slowing it to a stop. She lay the reins lightly in her lap, turning to look at her daughter with kind, knowing eyes.

"I know that it is hard to put away vanity, especially when you are still so young," she said.

"But you say that Henry is your friend -- does that mean you respect him?"

Mildred sat up straighter in her seat, her eyes wide.

"Ja, of course, I do," she said. "He is a gut man."

Her mother nodded, watching her with eyes filled with compassion. She reached across the seat and took Mildred's hand, squeezing it lightly.

"Then why do you think so little of him? From what you say, you are assuming that he would be so vain that he couldn't see a person's worth past their outward appearance."

Mildred slumped slightly in her seat, letting her mother's words sink into her.

She truly did think that Henry was a gut and Gottly man. He was respectful and kind, with a love of Gott and his community that showed in everything he did.

Why did she just assume that he could never love a woman like her?

"Do you think that you are placing your own vanity and insecurities on him?"

She blinked, letting this thought sink in. Was her vanity causing her to doubt her first true friend in Berlin?

Her mother smiled and squeezed her hand, before letting it go to pick up the reins once more. She flicked them lightly, steering the horse back out onto the road. The movement of the buggy fell back into the familiar rhythm as it trundled down the road and Mildred swayed lightly in the seat as she thought about what her mother had said.

"One thing is certain," her mother said, glancing over at Mildred. "You need to place all of this at Gott's feet and pray about it. He will guide you best."

Chapter Ten

Lavina sat down heavily on the sofa, letting out a gusty sigh as she sank into the cushions. Jacob was finally asleep -- he was teething, poor thing, and had been fussy for most of the afternoon and evening.

It had been quite a battle to get him to fall asleep, and after a long day, Lavina was feeling very worn out. She glanced over to where Samuel sat in his favorite armchair, a periodical on herbal remedies spread out in his lap.

The oil lamp flickered on the table beside him, casting long shadows across the floor as the sky outside began to darken.

After a few quiet moments, Samuel glanced up at his wife and smiled. He set the paper down on his lap, running a hand through his thick hair, that she had loosened from her kapp.

"You look just as tired as I feel," he chuckled.

Lavina smiled, tucking her feet up beneath her skirt as she reclined further into the cushions of the sofa. She loved these quiet moments with Samuel when Jacob was asleep and the house was silent. It felt gut to sit with him, even if they didn't talk much. Just being together was wonderful.

"I am tired," she admitted, stifling a yawn. "But it's a gut sort of tired, the kind you get after a gut day of work. You know that I like to be busy."

"The practice was much busier today than it has been all week," Samuel said. "It's been a gut month -- I think tomorrow we should take stock of our inventory and see what remedies and tinctures need to be made. It looked like we were running low on several things when I was shutting everything up for the day."

Lavina nodded, happy to help Samuel in anything he needed help with.

She yawned again and then grinned sheepishly as Samuel laughed gently at her.

"Why don't you go up to bed? I'm just going to finish reading this and then I'll be up," he said.

"Nee, I think I'll sit with you a bit if you don't mind," she said. "My mind is still whirling and I need to settle it down. It's nice to sit quietly for a bit."

Samuel sent her a look of affection and then picked up the periodical again. They sat quietly, Samuel reading silently and Lavina enjoying the sounds of the night outside the living room windows.

It was getting colder in the evenings and the feeling that snow was coming was starting to become stronger.

All the old-timers were saying there would be a storm sometime soon, and Lavina found herself welcoming the winter this year. It felt like a perfect bookend to a lovely year -- Christmas was coming up soon and she was looking forward to spending quality time with both of their families.

After several more moments, Samuel finally began to fold up his paper and set it on the table next to the oil lamp. He scrubbed lightly at his eyes with his hand, rolling his shoulders slightly as he eased the tension from his muscles.

"Mildred Lehman was in today while you were tending Jacob," he said, his eyes closed as he leaned his head back on the chair. "She is improving greatly -- though I'm not sure she sees it."

"Poor thing," Lavina breathed, shaking her head lightly. "If only she could gain some confidence in herself -- she has really allowed her injuries to affect her sense of self. It's such a shame. I've been trying to figure out some way to show her that life is still there for the taking even if she does have scars."

Samuel sat up slightly and looked at her, his eyebrows raised.

"What have you been scheming?"

Lavina laughed, waving a hand at him with affection. Her husband knew her too well for her to ever think she could get anything by him, not that she would ever want to.

"Who said I've been scheming? I'm merely trying to make sure that Mildred knows her worth."

Samuel continued to look at her with shrewd eyes and Lavina finally sighed, laughing as she threw up her hands in defeat. She had been meaning to talk her ideas over with Samuel the next day, but she supposed there was no time like the present.

"Fine, fine," she laughed. "I'll tell you my plan. I told you that I've been asked to help put together the artisan competition at the County Fair next week?"

Samuel nodded, sitting up slightly at the mention of the fair. It was a favorite event for all of the community and everyone was looking forward to it.

"I've decided that Mildred just must enter her knitting -- all those beautiful things she makes and sells at the coffee shop," Lavina said excitedly, clapping her hands together. "The winner of the competition gets a dinner for two at Miller's Diner and a lovely gift basket. Wouldn't that be perfect for Mildred?"

"A gift basket?" Samuel looked skeptically at his wife, unsure where she was going with this plan.

"Nee, silly," Lavina chuckled. "The dinner! Mildred could take someone on a date!"

"Lavina, honey," Samuel said slowly, shaking his head. "Mildred can't even bring herself to take that shawl off from around her head and kapp -- how is she going to go on a date?"

Lavina grinned, bouncing lightly on the sofa cushion as her eyes sparkled with excitement.

"I'm going to fill the judging panel with all of the eligible bachelors in town," she said excitedly. "I'll bribe them with baked guts and coffee. They'll see Mildred's knitting and be blown away by her skill and creativity. She's sure to win!"

Samuel still looked skeptical.

"And how does that turn into a date for Mildred?"

"She'll be so surprised that she won, and it will give her a much-needed boost of confidence," Lavina said, her voice sure. "And I'll be there to insist that she has to use that dinner-for-two prize, and I'll hint strongly that one of the nice young men who voted for her would make a lovely dinner companion for a bright young maedel like her."

Samuel's brows were still raised and he laughed ruefully.

"Lavina, you know that I love you," he said, shaking his head. "But that is the most half-baked plan I have ever heard. If that's your matchmaking efforts, maybe you should stick to healing and mothering."

Lavina threw one of the throw cushions at him, laughing as he caught it neatly in the air. She shook her finger playfully at him, laughing as he tossed the cushion back onto the sofa.

"Just you wait," she said. "It will work and Mildred will get a husband out of it. You'll see!"

Chapter Eleven

Henry set the last crate of milk bottles onto the large prep table in the center of the kitchen with a grunt.

As always, he had saved his delivery to Berlin Beans for last, so that he would have a small window of time to enjoy a coffee and catch up with Marshall.

Wiping his hands lightly on his trousers, he rotated his right arm to relieve some tension -- there had been a lot of deliveries this morning, and while he was glad to see the business growing, he was thinking it might be time to talk to his father about hiring someone to help deliver.

He walked out of the kitchen and into the main front room of the coffee shop, waving to one of the women behind the counter with a friendly smile.

He scanned the room, seeing that one of his favorite tables by the window was open, and made his way over. As he pulled out a chair, someone called his name.

"Henry! Gut to see you, friend," Marshall called as he came out of the back office. "Are you having your usual this morning?"

Henry raised a hand in greeting, nodding to his friend. Marshall shot him a grin and walked behind the counter to pour them both a cup of strong, dark coffee.

He approached the table with the two steaming mugs in hand, setting them down carefully on the table.

As he sat in the seat across from Henry, he smiled as the other man took a careful sip.

"Did your deliveries go well this morning?"

Henry swallowed his coffee, setting the mug back on the table.

"They did! But there were quite a few new stops this week," he said.

"I think I need to plan to sit down with my father and speak with him about possibly hiring some of the young men in the community to help. It would be gut part-time work for some of the teenagers, and would give them something to do."

Marshall nodded, glancing over at his young employees behind the counter.

"It's a gut feeling to be able to give them respectable work," he said. "I think your Daedd knows that and it sounds like a gut idea. I'm glad to see business booming for you! We've been busy too. I've been talking with Caleb about purchasing a second espresso machine to meet demand."

Caleb Miller was Marshall's business partner and another gut friend of Henry. Almost as if the sound of his name had summoned him, the bell over the door rang as Caleb stepped into the coffee shop.

He stamped his feet on the threshold rug, shrugging off his coat as the door swung shut behind it. He noticed Marshall and Henry as he hung his coat on the rack by the door, and lifted a hand in greeting. He mimed drinking a coffee and walked over to the counter.

Once Caleb had poured himself a mug of coffee, he sauntered over to their table and pulled out a chair.

"Gut dag, you two! And how goes it on this freezing winter morning?"

Marshall laughed, clapping a hand on his friend's back.

"If you think this is freezing, I pity you when it gets really cold," he chuckled.

"Gott made me for much warmer climates," Caleb pouted playfully, laughing as his friends rolled their eyes. "But really, it is gut to see you, Henry! I feel like we always miss each other when you're in the shop."

The three friends chatted amiably as they drank their coffee, sharing news of the community and beyond. Customers came into the shop, the sound of their voices and the noises from the kitchen creating a comforting din.

After a while, the bell above the door rang again, and Henry glanced over just in time to see Mildred duck in.

Her shawl was still pulled tight around her head, and she left it on as she slipped gracefully out of her wool cloak.

She had a basket over one arm, so he assumed she was here to restock her wares.

As she walked over to the shelves, Marshall called out a greeting and she waved happily to the men as they sat at their table. Henry waved back, feeling a tightening in his chest as he watched her.

He wished that she would take the shawl from her head so that he could see her face. He imagined that her cheeks were probably flushed from the cold, and her eyes would be bright.

When he looked back at his friends, they were both watching him shrewdly. Caleb looked like he was about to say something, but Henry cut him off.

"I need a refill," he said quickly, not really knowing why his cheeks were heating with a blush. "I'll be right back."

He jumped up from the table and sidled over to the counter. He waited for the tourists at the register to finish their orders and pay.

Once they had gone off to find a table, he handed his cup to the waitress and then wandered over to stand beside Mildred's shelf as she worked.

"Gut dag, Mildred," he said, smiling warmly at her and chuckling when she jumped slightly in surprise. "Looks like business has been gut for you, too! We were just talking about how busy we have all been."

She nodded, smiling back at him. The fleeting glimpse he caught of her smile from beneath her shawl made his heart skip a beat.

"It has been gut," she said, her voice soft but happy. "It keeps me busy and I love being able to help Maemm pay for the shopping."

Henry caught himself staring intently at Mildred, admiring her flashing dark eyes and graceful hands. He looked away, blushing, and cleared his throat.

"Would you care to join me for breakfast? I was thinking of buying a pastry or two," he said.

She stiffened slightly, pausing as she placed a knitted bag on the shelf. After a moment, she shook her head slowly.

"Nee, denke," she breathed, stepping back from the shelf. She wouldn't meet his eyes, and Henry felt as if he must have said something wrong.

"My mother is waiting for me," she said, her voice rushed. "I'll see you next time, Henry. Have a gut day."

Henry watched, bewildered, as she rushed to the door. She caught up her cloak, throwing it around her shoulders, and then slipped out the door.

The waitress sat his coffee on the counter and he picked it up, walking back to his table with a furrowed brow.

"Mildred darted out of here rather quickly," Marshall said, his voice questioning. "What did you say to frighten the poor girl off?"

"Nothing! I just asked if she wanted to join me for breakfast," Henry said confusedly.

"She's a friendly little thing," Caleb said. "But a bit strange."

Marshall nodded, glancing over at the shelves.

"She's so talented, her work never stays on the shelf long," he said. "But I can't help wondering if she is hiding something. Why is she always so bundled up? And why is her face always covered?"

Henry shrugged, trying to be nonchalant when he had wondered the same thing for weeks.

"Maybe she has one of those port-wine birthmarks on her face," Caleb said. "And that's why she always has a shawl pulled up to cover her because she's ashamed of the way she looks."

Henry shook his head vehemently.

"But that's ridiculous! Nee one cares what a maedel looks like if she's an interesting person and easy to talk to..."

He trailed off, his voice quieting as he saw the incredulous looks his friends were giving him. Suddenly, he felt very exposed. Setting down his coffee cup, he pushed his chair back and stood up.

"Denke for the kaffe," he said gruffly. "I need to get going so I can talk to my father about hiring some extra help."

As he walked quickly out of the coffee shop, he didn't miss the knowing looks on both of his friends' faces.

Chapter Twelve

"Oh, Mildred, before you go, can you fill out this form for the County Fair artisan contest?"

Lavina walked over to where Mildred sat in the healing practice back room, having just finished her most recent treatment session with Samuel. She smiled as the older girl bounced over, a piece of paper in her hands.

She was still a little surprised at herself for having the courage to enter the competition, but Lavina's excitement was infectious. Plus, she knew it would be great exposure for her little business.

She took the paper and pen that Lavina held out to her and set them on the table next to her. As she filled out the form, she half-listened as Lavina chattered away beside her.

"What have you decided to enter into the competition?"

"I've narrowed it down to three things," Mildred said, her eyes still on the paper in front of her. "I've been perfecting a new pattern stitch I designed earlier this year and I'll showcase that in a sweater. And then a nice soft basket for gifting and display, and a stuffed cow that looks like my Daedd's favorite old milker, Molly."

She smiled to herself as she remembered her father's pleased reaction when she had shown him the cow she had been working on.

"Oh, those all sound perfect," Lavina exclaimed. "The perfect way to show all of the unique items you create. And just think, after the competition you will be able to put "prize-winning" on all of your tags and business cards!"

Mildred laughed at her friend's enthusiasm. Lavina had proven to be a big supporter and cheerleader for her, and she was endlessly grateful for her. She had been worried about finding close female friendships when she had moved to Berlin, but Lavina had shown her that even with her injuries she was still capable of being a gut friend.

"Don't put the cart before the horse," she laughed, shaking her head affectionately. "There are bound to be many other talented artisans at the fair, and it will be stiff competition."

Lavina reached out and gripped her arm, giving it a light squeeze.

"You have a very gut chance of winning, Mildred," she said. "The judges will see your talent."

Mildred smiled as she finished filling out the form, handing it back to her friend.

"Nee matter what happens," she said. "It will have been an interesting experience. I'm looking forward to it!"

Lavina grinned, bouncing a little in excitement.

"Me too! It will be such a fun day," she said. "Will you ride with us to the fair? You'll need to come a bit earlier to set up your entries, and your parents can come later when the judging is scheduled."

Mildred nodded with a smile.

"Ja, that sounds perfect," she said. "I'll walk over and meet you when it is time to go."

She gave her friend a quick hug, pulling her shawl over her head as she walked out

The late afternoon sun was starting to dip below the tree line and the temperature had dropped several degrees since she had walked to the Mast home for her appointment. Mildred pulled her cloak tighter around herself and breathed in deeply.

She enjoyed the quiet walks to and from her treatment appointments, it gave her time to be quiet and reflective and to enjoy nature. It made her feel gut to be out in Gott's world, without having to worry who might see her scars.

Her mind wandered as she walked, and eventually came around to thinking about Henry.

She had seen him several times in the last few weeks, and she was thankful that things had gone back to normal between them since that disastrous morning when he had offered to buy her breakfast. She had frozen in panic at his offer, so sure that it would lead him to see her face more clearly.

She was still convinced that the minute Henry saw her scars, he would run for the hills.

There was nee way that such a handsome man would be attracted to someone as disfigured as she was. She knew that her mother thought she did Henry a disservice, assuming that he would be so shallow -- but she couldn't help it.

She knew that Henry was one of the best men that she knew, not only in looks but in character too. He deserved the best woman by his side, someone who could help him and love him but would also be someone he could be proud to stand beside.

If it were her, she would always wonder if he truly thought she deserved to be standing beside him.

Mildred shook her head, trying to dispel those thoughts. As if she would ever even come close to being the type of woman Henry might be interested in! Nee, Gott had other plans for her, she was sure of it.

She would spend her days building her small business and helping her parents supplement their own income with her earnings.

And when she was older, she would find herself a small cottage and take in boarders to make ends meet.

She would be the respectable unmarried aunt to all of her relations and friends. With a firm nod, she continued to trudge home.

She had the artisan market to look forward to, and a holiday season full of new friends. Lavina had been telling her about all of the fun events the community took part in centering around the Christmas holidays -- there would be community baking days and quilting bees, Sunday Singing gatherings and potlucks.

She would be very busy this season, and wouldn't have any time to stop and feel sorry for herself. Her life was wonderful! Gott had blessed her beyond imagining, even if she did have scars.

But even as she tried to convince herself, she still felt a kernel of doubt. It was one thing to tell yourself that Gott loved you just the way you were, scars and all, and quite another thing to believe that everyone else did too.

She knew that her vanity was a sin, and she prayed about it nightly. But it was so hard to overcome. Her mother would tell her to keep praying, and to lay it all out for Gott. And she would keep doing that, over and over until it stuck.

The wind whipped up the hillside, cutting through her cloak with ease. She shivered, tugging it closed and keeping her hands tucked inside the voluminous wool folds. The sun was almost completely covered by the tree line, and little lights of oil lamps were flickering on in the windows of the houses she passed. She came to a sharp bend in the road, where she would turn to walk up toward her house.

As she walked up the gravel drive, her boots crunching over the gravel, she offered up a silent, fervent prayer to Gott. Please, Lord, let Henry find a wife who deserves him. Someone who will help him and support him, someone who will take care of him and be the partner in life that someone of his character deserves.

Chapter Thirteen

Samuel pulled the buggy into the crowded parking lot, tugging lightly on the reins to slow the horse down as they slowed to a walk behind the buggy in front of them.

A sea of white tents was being erected in the field beyond the parking lot as people bustled about in the morning sun. The air was crisp and cool, with a cloud-filled sky. Lavina shielded her eyes from the glare and glanced worriedly at a line of dark clouds on the horizon.

"I hope it doesn't storm this weekend," she murmured, steadying herself on the seat as the buggy rocked lightly. "Everyone has worked so hard to make this the best fair in years, it would be such a shame if the weather turned."

Beside her, Samuel shook his head lightly. He raised a hand in greeting to someone he knew in the parking lot, and then glanced at his wife.

"It doesn't smell like snow," he said, grinning as his wife raised her eyebrows at him. "And none of the old men have said it's going to storm, so I think we are safe. What do you think, Mildred?"

Mildred pulled her shawl tighter around her face, smiling softly as she watched the couple from her perch on the back seat. She shrugged, glancing out at the sky.

"My Daedd is usually pretty gut at predicting the weather, and he didn't say anything."

Lavina let out a gusty sigh, sitting back on the bench.

"I hope you both are right," she said. "I'll just keep praying the weather holds."

Samuel deftly maneuvered the buggy into a parking space and pulled the reins to bring the horse to a stop.

He jumped down from the buggy to tie the horse to the hitching post and then came around to open the passenger door.

He helped Lavina down and then held his hand out for Mildred. As he helped the younger girl down, Lavina spun in place as she took in the fairgrounds with a smile.

"It's going to be such a fun day! Look at everyone," she exclaimed, tugging her cloak around her shoulders. She walked over to Mildred and took a basket from her, smiling at the younger girl. "Let's get you over to the artisan tent so you can set everything up -- I need to make sure everyone is in their proper place and the judges will be arriving on time."

Samuel walked over and kissed Lavina quickly on the cheek, grinning at the two women as he straightened.

"I had better go find where I'm supposed to be," he said. "Abner Mast has me running around today like I'm his apprentice again! Whoever decided it was a gut idea to put a retired man in charge of things didn't realize how seriously he would take it, I think he's missed bossing people around."

Lavina laughed and swatted playfully at her husband. He gave them both a jaunty wave and then sauntered off into the crowd.

Lavina turned to Mildred with a smile, adjusting her hold on the basket and gesturing for the younger girl to follow.

They walked through the tents, glancing to either side as both Amish and Englisch families set up booths for food and wares.

The smell of cooking food and baked guts mingled with the smell of freshly mowed grass, and the air was full of chattering voices.

It was a bustling, churning crowd and Lavina could tell that it was slightly overwhelming for Mildred. The younger girl was looking around her with wide eyes.

As they approached the artisan tent, Lavina pointed toward a booth several yards down the center aisle that ran the length of the tent.

"That one is yours! There's a wood table to display your pieces and a chair for you to sit in," she said, steering Mildred over. "I need to go make sure everyone is finding their spots, but I'll check on you in a bit!"

She set the basket she was carrying down on the table and squeezed Mildred's arm. The younger girl smiled, tugging her shawl tighter around her face.

She began to unpack her basket, unwrapping each beautiful knitting item with care. Lavina frowned as she turned away -- she wished there was some way to get Mildred's confidence back. She truly hoped this experience would help her realize that she was so much more than her scars.

~ ~ ~ ~ ~

Lavina stepped to the side of the tent, wiping her face with a handkerchief. It had been a busy morning directing artisans and judges, but the Fair was now open and the crowds were trickling in.

She breathed a sigh of relief, looking around at the colorful displays in each booth with pride. There really were some beautiful guts on display this year -- and she was so happy that she had been able to extend the judging categories so that each artisan truly had a gut chance at winning the prizes.

It was the first year for the Fair to have a dedicated Quilting category, which meant that the other needlework artists had a much better chance.

She walked past several booths as she made her way to Mildred.

She stopped to admire a woodworker and quilter, lingering over a booth that displayed brightly colored jars of jams and preserves. But soon she was at Mildred's booth, and she smiled as she caught sight of the beautiful knitted items.

Mildred sat in her chair, pulled as far back into her small booth as possible. The shawl was still covering her face, and her cloak was around her shoulders. She looked like a small, wizened old woman and not the vibrant, intelligent young maedel she truly was. Lavina shook her head -- this wouldn't do! The judges were on their way over and Mildred needed to be front and center behind her table.

She stalked over to the younger girl and smiled wide as she approached. Mildred started with surprise, her eyes wide beneath her shawl.

"Mildred! You must get up! The judges are on their way over," Lavina said brightly, grabbing the younger girl's arm and pulling her to her feet. She walked Mildred over to the table and linked her arm with hers.

A small group of young Amish men ambled down the row between booths, stopping at each one to look things over.

They each held a clipboard and were taking notes as they looked. Lavina grinned, bouncing with excitement.

"They are sure to love your work," she whispered, smiling at Mildred. "And aren't they all so handsome? I wonder which one you will win the dinner with! Oh, it's so exciting!"

Mildred's eyes grew wide as the group came closer, and she seemed to shrink in on herself. Lavina shook her head, shaking the younger girl's arm lightly.

"None of that! You worked hard on these things," she whispered fiercely. "You are a talented maedel, and you should stand proudly at this table!"

As the men approached, she pushed Mildred lightly forward until the younger girl was gripping the edge of the table.

One of the men looked intently over the knitted items displayed on the table before glancing up at Mildred.

"Did you make all of these yourself?"

She nodded, her eyes wide. Lavina nudged her lightly, brows raised, and Mildred cleared her throat.

"J-Ja, I did," she said, her voice soft.

"This sweater is especially fine," one of the other men said, touching the sweater lightly. "What stitch is this? I don't think I've ever seen it before."

"I created the stitch myself," Mildred said, her voice growing a bit stronger with each word.

The men all looked at her with interest, their interest piqued. As they asked questions about each piece, Lavina watched happily as Mildred answered steadily. When it came to her work, the younger girl really did come into her own.

Chapter Fourteen

Henry stood from his crouch, pressing his hands into his lower back as he stretched lightly. It had been a busy morning of setting up their booth at the fair -- but it had been gut work, he decided, as he looked around at their display of cheese, cream, and butter with pride.

His father and mother were still bustling around, making sure everything could be seen from the front of the booth.

Henry had offered to help rather than staying back with his brothers to oversee the dairy, and he was hoping to have a few moments to go and see Mildred.

He was hoping that at some time today he could bring her to meet his parents, and maybe his father could talk to her a bit about dairy farming and cows.

Henry had mentioned some of the girl's ideas and experience to his father, and the older man had been interested. He also just wanted to see her -- it had been a week or so since their last meeting, and he found that he missed talking with her.

"Daedd, would you mind if I ducked away for a bit to visit with Mildred Lehman? I think she is in the next tent over," he said, smiling as his father moved a cheese wheel several millimeters to the right.

The older man glanced up and smiled at his son, nodding as he cut his eyes to his wife.

"That's nee problem, Henry," he said, with a knowing smile. "See if you can get the maedel to sneak away for a bit, your mother and I would like to meet her."

Henry blushed lightly, nodding his head as he made his way out into the row that ran between booths. As he exited one tent and entered another, his eyes widened at the brightly colored displays of the artisan tent.

He admired the items as he walked, his eyes roaming over every booth. As he looked ahead, he noticed Lavina Graber standing at the edge of a booth with her hands clasped in front of her. She bounced lightly with excitement, and as Henry looked beyond her he could see why.

Mildred stood behind a table of knitted objects, her shawl still wrapped around her face despite the fact that they were inside a large tent. A group of men stood in front of the table, their eyes trained on the items displayed. Henry walked towards the booth, coming up to stand alongside Lavina.

"Oh! Henry! Come to see Mildred's display?"

Lavina smiled kindly at him and he grinned in return.

"Wouldn't miss it for the world," he said. "How is everything going?"

"They seem to be very interested in the sweater," she whispered excitedly. "I think it's a big plus that she created the stitch herself. And David has already tried to buy that knit cow for his nephew, so there's that!"

Henry chuckled, his eyes on the judges. They were all young men, and he realized that all of them were unmarried and beardless.

Wasn't the prize for the artisan categories a dinner for two at the diner? Would one of these men be who Mildred chose to accompany her?

The thought of Mildred going to dinner with another man ripped through him painfully, and Henry blinked in surprise. That was unexpected! He shook the feeling off, promising himself to look more closely at it when he was alone. He turned his attention back to the judges, his eyes narrowing.

"What are they hemming and hawing for? Everyone can plainly see her work is the best," he said, his voice a low rumble.

Lavina glanced at him in surprise, her eyes narrowing in thought. Henry avoided her gaze, keeping his eyes trained on Mildred.

After several moments, the group of judges peeled away from the booth and moved to the center of the aisle. They conferred for several moments before one of them stepped a bit away from the group and held up a piece of paper with the words Third Place written in bold black ink.

Lavina made an excited sound as the man set the paper on a table holding crocheted boppoli blankets. Everyone clapped lightly as the woman behind the table flushed with pride.

Another man held up a sign that said Second Place and made his way over to a table with handsewn and embroidered handkerchiefs. As everyone clapped, Henry noticed that Mildred's shoulders drooped slightly.

He felt a growing sense of righteous indignation -- it was apparent to anyone with eyes and a brain that Mildred was the clear winner, but what if the judges had neither? What if they didn't like knitted things, or never wore sweaters? If Mildred didn't win, he would --- he would --

He would what? Henry shook himself lightly, surprised at the rush of indignation that had passed through him. He said a quick prayer to Gott that the judges would see what he could see, and then held his breath as one of them held up the First Place paper.

Lavina clasped his arm and bounced even faster as the man walked down the aisle, stopping in front of Mildred's table. With a flourish, he set the paper down on the sweater. Lavina gave a happy cry and rushed to her friend's side.

Henry grinned wildly, looking around happily as the crowd clapped raucously.

The judges all came over to congratulate Mildred, and as she walked around to the front of her table Henry noticed that her limp seemed more pronounced than usual. She must be tired, he thought to himself. Maybe he should offer to drive her home, and she could also meet his parents.

He walked over so that he could congratulate her and make his offer. She turned, her eyes catching his. She smiled, her hand coming up to wave at him, and Henry felt his heart squeeze. Just as he was about to congratulate her, the entrance to the tent blew open with a gust of wind.

The breeze sent table covers and cloaks fluttering, and Mildred's scarf slipped from around her face before anyone could blink. Henry saw her grab for it, and then it was gone.

As she turned after her shawl, Henry noticed for the first time that the side of her face was badly scarred. It looked like it was from some terrible burns, and his breath caught at the idea that she had ever been hurt that badly.

He stepped forward, the shock coursing through him. She turned back to him, and her eyes widened in fear and embarrassment. Henry tried to school his expression back to a friendly smile, and he walked over to pick up her shawl.

He handed it to her, a smile still on his face. But she wouldn't meet his eyes, merely taking the shawl from him with shaking fingers. She wound it around her head, pulling it tightly around her face. As Henry took a step toward her, she looked at him with large, wounded eyes and then turned and fled.

"Mildred!"

He called after her, but she slipped out of the tent and was gone.

Chapter Fifteen

Mildred ran blindly from the Fair tent, clutching her shawl at her shoulders. She dodged through the crowd of people, bursting out into the early afternoon sunshine.

Darting towards the road, she ran until her legs churned underneath her and her heart pounded wildly in her chest. She ran past the parking lot where all the buggies and horses were parked, and past the driveway onto the Fairgrounds.

She ran alongside the road the led back into town, her boots pounding on the roadside gravel until a sharp stitch in her side made her have to slow to a walk.

She stifled a sob, feeling the pain and humiliation rip through her. She reached up and wiped the tears from her flushed face, wanting to scream in frustration.

She was thankful that it seemed like everyone was at the Fair because the road was empty of vehicles and buggies. She knew she must look an absolute fright -- her thick hair was long and wild, escaping from beneath her kapp.

Her shawl, which was normally wrapped tightly around her head, was now draped haphazardly around her shoulders. She was flushed and breathing heavily, out of breath and wanting to cry.

Everything that she had feared had happened! And she couldn't believe that it had all happened so publicly.

The look on Henry' face when he had seen her scars -- shock and dismay -- flashed across her conscious and she cringed.

She was positive that everyone else in that tent probably looked the same, staring horrified at the disfigured girl before them. She shook her head wildly, trying to dispel the image of Henry staring at her in disgust.

She pulled her shawl tighter around her shoulders, considering if she should stop and wrap it once again around her face. But what was the point now?

Everyone had seen her, and everything was ruined. The humiliation was more than she could bear.

The sound of buggy wheels and the clip-clop of a horses' hooves approaching from behind made her step to the side of the road, ducking her head, she kept her face hidden.

She slowed her walk, waiting for the buggy to pass, but was dismayed when it slowed down beside her.

Glancing over she felt her heart drop to her toes. Henry sat in the driver's seat, an older woman on the bench beside him. They were both watching her with concerned expressions.

Henry reached across and gripped the passenger window. "Let me drive you back, Mildred," he called, his voice kind and warm. "You've left behind your prizes and all of the beautiful things you made for the Fair."

She shook her head, not meeting his eyes.

"Nee, denke," she said, trying to keep her voice steady. She made the mistake of glancing up, and she saw that the older woman had a look of such extreme empathy and kindness that Mildred felt the tears well again in her eyes.

Henry said something softly to his companion, and then he opened the drivers' side door. Hopping down, he rounded the buggy and walked over to her. He stood an arms-length away, his expression worried.

"Come on, Mildred," he said softly. "Let us give you a ride. If not back to the fair, then let us take you home. It's not gut for you to be out here walking along this busy road all alone, and it's too long of a distance for you to walk."

"I said, nee, denke," Mildred said shortly, still not meeting his eyes. She turned away, taking several steps away from him down the road.

"I didn't realize you were such an unkind woman," he said, his voice turning hard. "To pretend not to even know a friend who offers a kindness."

Mildred felt a spark of irritation and whirled to face him, her cloak fanning out from her body. She pushed her hair away from her face, bearing her scars to his view.

"I saw your expression," she exclaimed, trying to keep the hurt from her voice. "It was written all over your face!"

Henry' hard expression softened a bit and he took a step forward, his hand coming up in a placating gesture.

"You saw surprise," he said. "And sadness that you were ever hurt so badly."

Mildred blinked, suddenly aware that he was very close. She stared up at him, her eyes wide, as his hand came up to gently cup her scarred cheek. The feeling of his palm against her face made her jump, and she tried to pull away but he grabbed hold of her arm.

"I thought that we were friends," he said softly, his voice rough with emotion. His grip on her arm softened, and he tugged her toward him. When she glanced up at him, he was staring down into her eyes with such intensity that it made her breath catch in her throat. "I look forward to seeing you in the kaffe shop. I like talking to you. I admire and respect you for your intelligence, and your talent."

Mildred felt the tears leaking from her eyes, and sliding down her ruined cheek.

"But I'm hideous," she sobbed. "I scare kinner with this face! I'm a monster."

Henry moved his hands to her shoulders, giving her a little shake.

"Then maybe some mothers need to educate their kinner better," he said, his voice soft but stern. "Maybe those kinner need to learn not to look at the outside of a person to see their worth."

He drew her even closer until she could tip her forehead forward until lightly touched the front of his shirt. They stood there, breathing quietly as Mildred struggled to regain control of her emotions.

"As for me, I'm tired of looking for a wife who doesn't fit into my life," Henry said softly, his voice a quiet rumble. "I want a woman who can keep up with my business idea, who has ideas of her own. Someone who is talented in her own right, and one who doesn't mind working with cows."

He chuckled softly, placing his hand below her chin and tipping her face up to look at him. Her eyes were shining through her tears, a faint flush spreading across her cheeks.

"And besides," he said with a soft laugh. "That sweater you knitted looks like it would be a perfect fit."

She blushed fully, a faint grin spreading across her lips.

"Well, I was thinking of giving it to you for Christmas," she said softly, her eyes sparkling up at him.

"I want the little knitted cow, too," he chuckled, earning a soft laugh. "Now, are you going to let me court you, or are you going to continue to cruelly pretend you don't know me?"

Mildred ducked her head, trying to hide the bright blush she knew was now spreading across her face. He gently raised her face again, and she caught sight of the older woman sitting in the buggy.

She was watching the young couple, a look of happiness on her face. Mildred realized she must be Henry mother, and the sight of her happy at her son's choice made a faint surge of confidence bloom within her.

"But won't you be ashamed to have someone who looks like me beside you?"

"Man looks on the outward appearance, but the Lord looks at the heart," Henry recited softly, his hand coming up to touch her cheek lightly. "And your heart has been the most beautiful thing I have ever seen since the very first day I met you."

The tears welled in Mildred's eyes and she gave a wrenching sob. Henry looked suddenly alarmed, tugging her to him until he could hug her gently.

"Hush, sweetheart," he said softly. "Did I say something wrong?"

Mildred shook her head against his shirt, struggling to stop her tears.

"Nee! I'm just so happy, I can barely stand it," she said, laughing through her tears. "I should have trusted Gott all along. This is His doing and it is beautiful!"

Chapter Sixteen

Lavina shaded her eyes against the glare of the sun, looking across the parking lot and toward the road. She stood at the entrance to the fairground, trying to see which way Mildred had gone. The poor dear had run out of the tent before anyone could stop her, and Lavina felt worry bubble up within her.

Footsteps behind her made her whirl around, and she felt relief when she saw her husband striding toward her.

"Oh, Samuel! What a mess," she cried. "Poor Mildred has run off, and I've nee idea where she could have gone."

Samuel came to stand beside her, reaching his arm out to wrap it around her waist.

"I heard what happened," he said, his brow furrowed. "She can't have gone far on foot. I'll go unhitch the buggy and see if she's headed down ——"

He cut off when Lavina made a frantic noise, bouncing on her feet beside him. She pointed across the parking lot, and Samuel watched as a buggy drove toward the Fairground.

"Why, that's Henry' Schrock's buggy! And look! Mildred is with him!"

Lavina watched, eyes wide, as the buggy parked nearby. Henry was in the driver's seat, with Mildred seated beside him. His mother, Mrs. Schrock, was on the backbench. All three looked happy as could be, and Lavina felt her curiosity spike.

Lavina and Samuel watched as Henry jumped down and rounded the buggy. He opened the passenger door and helped his mother down gently, making sure she was steady on her feet before turning to Mildred.

He reached out for her, lifting her from the buggy and setting her down with great care. The two young people had eyes only for each other, and Lavina heard Samuel chuckle lightly beside her.

"Well now, isn't that something?"

Lavina glanced at him with a grin.

Henry linked arms with Mildred and led her and his mother into the tent, the Grabers trailing behind. They headed straight for Mildred's booth, and Henry smiled at everyone they passed.

Lavina watched as the people around them whispered together, their eyes wide and their smiles big. It was plain to see that soon everyone would be hearing about the Schrock boy courting the Lehman maedel.

At the booth, Mildred began to pack away her wares with Henry's help. Lavina continued to watch the way the two of them interacted, and she was impressed by how gentle he was with Mildred.

How could she have been so wrong about him? He wasn't the vain young man she had assumed he would be, and the sight of the two of them together warmed her heart.

Henry walked Mildred over to where Samuel was standing and the three of them talked for a moment. Lavina sidled closer, catching the last of the conversation.

"We should see if we can get your father to see Samuel," he was saying, his gaze warm as he looked at Mildred. "He has helped you so much, just think of what he could do to help your Daedd."

Ja, Lavina thought to herself, *Henry Schrock is a gut man.*

Samuel came up beside her again and watched silently for a moment.

"Nee disappointment that your matchmaking scheme didn't work?"

Lavina grimaced lightly, giving a rueful chuckle.

"Oh, that," she sighed. "Just think of all the baked guts I wasted bribing all those eligible men to be judges!"

Samuel laughed, slinging an arm around her shoulders.

"Well, at least I know them all better now," she mused, leaning her head lightly on her husband's shoulder. "I should be able to match them with the perfect wives in nee time at all!"

At the sound of her husband's playful groan, she poked him in the side and the two laughed brightly as they watched the young couple walk hand in hand out of the Fair tent and out into the bright afternoon sun.

Epilogue

Mildred wiped her hand on her apron and walked to the back door, pushing open the screen door. She walked out onto the porch, shielding her eyes from the glare of the sun as she scanned the yard just behind the house.

Beyond the yard was a freshly painted barn framed by the green of the pastures beyond. A clutch of Guernsey cows, just bought a few weeks before, were standing beneath the shade of an oak tree. The sight made Mildred sigh with happiness, and she smiled as she caught sight of her husband as he walked out of the barn.

"Supper is ready," she called, waving as he approached the house.

Henry lifted a hand in return, and she thought how handsome he looked with his full beard framing his strong jaw. A wayward lock of hair caught the breeze, and she reached up to tuck it back into her bun. A wail from behind her inside the house made her turn, and she went back inside with a smile on her face.

Poor boppoli Betty was teething, and her miserable little cries could shake the entire house. Mildred went to get her from her crib and came back into the kitchen for a cold washcloth. As she pumped the water over the cloth with one hand, the boppoli propped on her hip, the back door opened and Henry came striding in.

He walked over and slung an arm around Mildred's shoulders, ducking to kiss her lightly on the cheek and the top of Betty's head.

"How are my two beautiful girls?"

The feel of Henry' kiss on her cheek made Mildred reach up, her fingers ghosting along the old scar tissue. It was so much better these days, after so many treatments with Samuel Graber.

It was still noticeable, but much softer than it had been.

But Mildred hardly noticed it at all, not since Henry had shown her that it had nee impact on how he saw her.

She wondered if Henry saw what Gott saw — only what was in her heart and her mind and not her scars. She stood there in her kitchen, her boppoli daughter wriggling against her and her loving husband standing close by, and she sent a silent prayer of thanks to Gott for all of His blessings.

As Henry began to serve them their supper, Mildred sat down at the table with Betty in her lap. She watched as Henry made funny faces to get the boppoli to laugh, and she felt a rush of joy at how easily he had fallen into the role of father. She was looking forward to a special dessert. She had made his favorite dessert from the pantry and surprise him with her news.

She had been feeling queasy in the mornings, and the healer had confirmed what she had suspected. Soon there would be another boppoli for Henry to spoil, just another of Gott's perfect blessings in her life.

THE END

~ ~ ~ ~ ~

.

A Free book

Would you like a free story?

Claim Amish Special Delivery Here

**https://dl.bookfunnel.com/t9mmo3b6
rs**

Printed in Great Britain
by Amazon

23502533R00086